Alison

the Art

Fairy

To Sarah B, a true friend

Special thanks to Rachel Elliot

Copyright © 2014 by Rainbow Magic Limited.

All rights reserved. Published by Scholastic Inc., *Publishers since 1920.* SCHOLASTIC and associated logos are trademarks and/or registered trademarks of Scholastic Inc. RAINBOW MAGIC is a trademark of Rainbow Magic Limited. Reg. U.S. Patent & Trademark Office and other countries. HIT and the HIT logo are trademarks of HIT Entertainment Limited.

The publisher does not have any control over and does not assume any responsibility for author or third-party websites or their content.

No part of this publication may be reproduced, stored in a retrieval system, or transmitted in any form or by any means, electronic, mechanical, photocopying, recording, or otherwise, without written permission of the publisher. For information regarding permission, write to Scholastic Inc., Attention: Permissions Department, 557 Broadway, New York, NY 10012.

ISBN 978-0-545-85206-7

10 9 8 7 6 5 4 3 2 1   16 17 18 19 20

Printed in the U.S.A.   40
First edition, July 2016

Alison

the Art
Fairy

by Daisy Meadows

SCHOLASTIC INC.

The Fairyland Palace

Fairyland School

Tippington Town

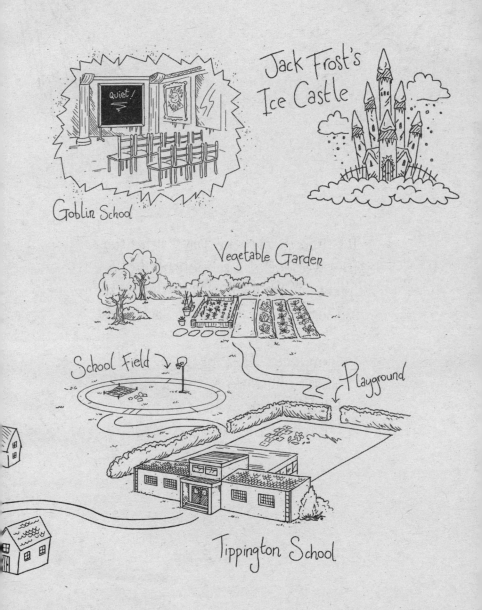

Goblin School

Jack Frost's Ice Castle

Vegetable Garden

School Field

Playground

Tippington School

It's time the School Day Fairies see
How wonderful a school should be—
A place where goblins must be bossed,
And learn about the great Jack Frost.

Now every fairy badge of gold
Makes goblins do as they are told.
Let silly fairies whine and wail.
My cleverness will never fail!

Contents

Best Friends Together

"Lunchtime already!" exclaimed Rachel Walker, closing her math book. "I wonder what kind of sandwiches Mom packed today."

"I can't believe I'm really here at school with you!" Kirsty Tate said with a smile.

Rachel nodded happily. Being in the same class as her best friend really was a dream come true! Kirsty normally went to school in Wetherbury, but heavy rain over the summer had flooded the classrooms. Now the school was closed for a week while the damage was repaired.

Mrs. Tate and Mrs. Walker had been chatting on the phone when Rachel came up with the idea of inviting Kirsty to Tippington. By the end of the call it was decided—Kirsty would stay with the Walkers for the week and go to school there. At first Kirsty had felt a little nervous about starting the school year somewhere new, but the thought of sitting next to her best friend in every class was so exciting! Since she'd started yesterday, she'd loved getting to know Rachel's school. Everybody had been really friendly, apart from the pair of naughty goblins that had joined the class pretending to be new boys! Only Kirsty and Rachel had figured out who the screeching voices, pointy noses, and green uniforms really belonged to.

"Get out of my way!" yelled one of them now, barging to the front of the class.

"Nope!" grunted the other. "I'm getting *my* lunch first!"

Kirsty's teacher, Mr. Beaker, frowned at the noisy pair.

"Settle down, please," he said sternly. "You'll cause an accident if you push and shove."

The goblins were fighting so loudly they didn't hear a word Mr. Beaker said. As they struggled to get through the door, they bumped into a table, knocking over a stack of cardboard boxes. Egg cartons, paper towel rolls, and empty tissue boxes tumbled all over the floor. Kirsty and Rachel rushed to pick them back up again.

"Those awful goblins!" whispered
Rachel. "I hope they don't cause any
more trouble."

Kirsty watched
the pair barge
out of the
room with
Mr. Beaker
on their
heels.

"I have
a horrible
feeling
they might," she
said ruefully.

During one of their first classes
together, the girls had met someone
amazing—Marissa the Science Fairy.
Kirsty and Rachel had been friends with

the fairies ever since their first trip to Rainspell Island. The girls were always ready to help them outwit Jack Frost and his army of goblin servants. This time, however, Jack Frost really had gone a step too far. He'd sent his goblins to steal four magical gold star badges belonging to the School Day Fairies— Marissa and her friends Alison the Art Fairy, Lydia the Reading Fairy, and Kathryn the Gym Fairy. He had a rotten plan in mind for the badges, too. The vain Jack Frost had set up his own school for goblins, filled with classes all about him!

The poor School Day Fairies had been dismayed. They needed their badges to make subjects interesting and help lessons run smoothly. Until the precious objects were back where they belonged, classes in Fairyland and the human world were in trouble.

"I don't want another science lesson like yesterday," said Rachel, giving a little shudder. The morning had been full of mishaps until Kirsty and Rachel had figured out what was happening. The rowdy new boys had turned out to be two of Jack Frost's naughtiest students, a pair so full of mischief that they'd even been expelled from his goblin school! Before leaving Jack Frost's frozen kingdom, the goblins had stolen all four magical badges and fled to the human world. Kirsty and Rachel had managed to return one badge to Marissa, but they still needed to find the other three.

"We have to be ready for anything,"

said Kirsty, picking up an armful of cardboard. "If the goblins are still in school, the badges must be here somewhere, too."

"But Marissa said that King Oberon and Queen Titania will be visiting the Fairyland School in a few days," remarked Rachel with a sigh. "We have to get the badges back before then."

"There isn't much time," agreed Kirsty.

"Time for what?"

The friends spun around. Mr. Beaker had walked back into the classroom! Rachel's cheeks turned red. She hoped that the teacher hadn't overheard their conversation—nobody else knew about the fairies. Before she could think of an answer, Kirsty piped up.

"I was just telling Rachel that it's time to go out to the playground!"

Mr. Beaker nodded, then sat down at his desk.

"Thanks for picking up those boxes, girls," he said gratefully.

"I've been collecting them all summer."

"What are they for?" Rachel wondered aloud.

Now Mr. Beaker was the one looking mysterious.

"It's for a special art project," was all he would say. "You'll find out more after lunch."

Kirsty and Rachel exchanged excited smiles. Art was one of their favorite subjects!

As soon as they'd eaten their sandwiches and fruit, Rachel took Kirsty out to the playground.

"Look, Amina and Adam are over there!" cried Rachel, pointing to her friends.

"Should we go say hello?" suggested Kirsty.

Amina and Adam were in a quiet

corner, kneeling side by side on the blacktop.

"Mr. Beaker said we could use chalk to create some playground art," explained Amina, "as long as we wash it off every Friday."

"Or it rains first!" Adam grinned, pointing up to the sky.

Amina handed a box of chalk to Rachel and Kirsty. "Want to try?"

The girls replied at once. "Yes, please!"

"I know just what to draw," declared Rachel, pulling out a piece of red chalk. "A fairy!"

She imagined Ruby the Red Fairy

fluttering in the sky.
She could just
picture the
shape of
her dainty
wings and
the rosebuds
in her hair.
Next to her,
Kirsty tipped out
the rest of the colors of chalk.

"Why don't I draw a rainbow for the
fairy to fly over?" she suggested.

Rachel beamed. She couldn't help but
notice the secret twinkle in Kirsty's eye!
Soon the girls' chalk picture began to
take shape.

"Something's not right," said Rachel,
standing back to look at it better.

Somehow Ruby's cheerful face had creased up into a frown! Her wand was crooked, too.

"My poor rainbow." Kirsty sighed. "It's turned into a smudgy mess!"

Amina and Adam weren't doing much better. They had tried to draw a happy farmyard scene, but it had just come out as scribbles.

"I don't want to do this anymore," said Adam, putting down the chalk and standing up. "Let's go play on the swings."

Amina followed him, leaving Rachel and Kirsty by themselves.

Rachel wrinkled her nose. "I would never draw Ruby without a smile," she remarked. "Do you think this has something to do with the missing badges?"

"Y-yes!" stuttered Kirsty, grabbing Rachel's arm and pointing down at her chalk rainbow.

Rachel gasped. The blurry pinks, yellows, and blues had started to shimmer and glow! A magical haze billowed over the ground, glinting with colorful twinkles. A tiny dot in the middle started to get bigger and bigger until . . . *ting*! A magical fairy appeared!

Puzzling Pictures

As soon as she spotted Kirsty and Rachel, the fairy did a happy twirl.

"Hello again!" she chimed in a singsong voice. "I'm so happy I found you!"

The fairy waved her wand with a flourish. A cloud of tiny artist's palettes instantly popped into the air around her. Each one was a perfect miniature,

complete with brushes and ovals of
brightly colored paint.

"We met yesterday, didn't we?" asked
Kirsty, remembering their trip to the
Fairyland School.

"You're Alison," added Rachel,
"Alison the Art Fairy!"

Alison giggled with pleasure. She really

did look as pretty as a picture. Her sunny
blond hair tumbled in waves around her
shoulders, topped off with a dusty pink
beret. She wore a bright, polka-dotted
T-shirt with a slogan on it, jangly beads,
and a maxi skirt in different shades of pink.

"It's tie-dyed," she said proudly when
she noticed Kirsty and Rachel admiring
her skirt. "I made it myself!"

The cheerful little fairy was full of
chatter until the messy chalk drawings
on the ground caught her eye.

"Oh dear," she said forlornly. "You
can probably guess why I'm here."

Kirsty glanced nervously over her
shoulder, then knelt down next to Alison.

"Is it your gold star badge?" Kirsty
whispered.

Alison nodded furiously.

"I really need to get it back. My magical badge makes sure that all art lessons are full of fun and go smoothly! Imagine a world without beautiful drawings, paintings, and sculptures! What a terrible, gloomy thought . . ."

With that, the fairy's voice trailed off. Rachel glimpsed the tiniest silver tear trickle down Alison's cheek.

"We'll put things right," she replied kindly. "The goblins can't get away with this!"

Kirsty took Rachel's hand, her face full of determination.

"We'll find your badge in no time," she promised.

Alison's face brightened at once. But before she could say another word, a group of children ran past.

"You need to hide," whispered Rachel. "Can you fly into my pocket?"

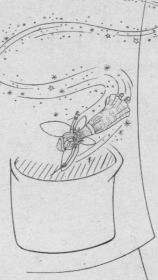

Quick as a flash, Alison darted into Rachel's jacket pocket and ducked out of sight. A trail of tiny stars glittered in the air behind her for just a second, disappearing one by one.

Kirsty and Rachel waited as more of their classmates galloped past them. A big circle of children had formed on the other side of the playground. Even Adam and Amina had stopped swinging and joined the crowd.

"What's happening over there?" asked
Rachel, catching Amina's arm.

"It's the new boys," she answered
breathlessly. "Come and see what
they've done!"

"Is it something against the rules?"
guessed Kirsty.

"Oh no," replied Adam. "They made
the most amazing chalk drawing ever!"

Kirsty raised an eyebrow at Rachel.

"The goblins are up to something already," she said, just loudly enough for Alison to hear.

Kirsty and Rachel grabbed their backpacks and ran over to get a better look.

"What do you think?" squawked one of the goblins, seeing their curious faces. "Better than your silly scribbles, isn't it?"

"Who'd want to draw a fairy, anyway?" barked the other one. "Our drawings are the best!"

For once, the goblins were absolutely right. The blacktop was covered with the most eye-catching, astonishing chalk art the girls had ever seen.

"It's Jack Frost's Ice Castle!" said Rachel. Every detail was perfect. The castle had

spiky turrets, frosty
icicles, and a
forbidding
oak door. The
picture glistened
in blues, whites,
and silvers,
creating a feeling so
wintry it made Kirsty shiver.

"Look," she whispered under her
breath, "they've even added the new
goblin school. There's the playground on
the side."

"No goblin could have drawn this on
his own," added Rachel.

"They must have Alison's gold star
badge with them right now!" Kirsty
replied urgently.

Kirsty gazed at the two smug goblins

bragging about their handiwork. Although the other children didn't recognize the Ice Castle, they couldn't help but be impressed by the glittering colors and intricate shapes. Kirsty edged a little closer to the bigger and more boastful goblin.

"I'll sign autographs if you want," he was crowing to the crowd, "but only if you give me some candy!"

Kirsty blinked. She was sure she could see the tip of the magical badge poking out of his green pants pocket!

"I think I can get it," she mouthed to Rachel, reaching out her hand.

Kirsty's fingers trembled as she got closer and closer to the badge. Rachel held her breath . . .

A Sticky Situation

Rrrinnnggg!

Quick as a flash, Kirsty pulled back her hand. The goblin with the magical badge groaned as the children picked up their backpacks and drifted away.

"Don't go!" he yelled. "Watch me draw something else. Look at how awesome I am!"

"That's the bell for the end of lunch,"
said Rachel firmly. "We have to go back
to class."

The goblin blew
a raspberry at her
and followed his
friend inside. The
naughty pair
didn't even bother
picking up their
chalk before they left.

"I was so close," Kirsty
said when she and Rachel got back
inside. Alison peeked out of her hiding
place.

"It was a very good try," she said
cheerfully. "If that bell had rung a second
later, you would definitely have gotten
my badge back."

Rachel gave Kirsty's hand an encouraging squeeze. "At least we know where the badge is now," she said. "We just have to outsmart those goblins."

Alison pointed her wand down the hall. "Time to hide again," she reminded them. "Mr. Beaker is starting the lesson."

When Kirsty and Rachel walked back into the classroom, there was an excited buzz in the air. Mr. Beaker had covered the tables with old newspapers and laid out glue, scissors, and paintbrushes. In the middle of every table he'd also stacked interesting piles of old boxes and cardboard tubes.

The children laughed and chatted as they put on their art aprons. Some picked up the boxes on their tables and started to play with them. Across the room, the silly goblins were using paper-towel tubes as pretend swords, then bashing each other on the head.

"They're making mischief already," warned Kirsty. "Look."

Mr. Beaker clapped his hands three times, then waited for everybody to settle down.

"This afternoon I'm giving you an art challenge," he announced. "Every table should work together as a group. You have one hour to use the cardboard boxes in the middle to make a model vehicle. The group who makes the best one will get a gold star, and the vehicle will be put on display for the school superintendent's visit in two days."

The teacher held up a model of a car that he'd made earlier.

"I glued this together myself, then painted the outside with blue paint," he continued. "I bet you can come up with something even more creative . . . Oh!"

Before Mr. Beaker could finish talking, the car's wheels dropped off! One by one, all four of the disks went tumbling across the classroom.

"I don't know what happened there," he muttered, sitting down to get a better look at the little car. At the same moment, the pile of extra boxes on the desk beside him fell over. Mr. Beaker winced as an empty egg carton bounced off his head. *Bop!*

The goblins roared with laughter. Their hoots got even louder when the egg carton landed on top of Mr. Beaker's model car, breaking it into pieces.

"How strange," the teacher mumbled

to himself, looking sad. "I'm sure it was glued properly . . ."

"Are you all right, Mr. Beaker?" asked Rachel.

"Yes, thank you," he replied. "OK, class, time to get started."

Kirsty and Rachel were in a group with Adam and Amina. They passed around the boxes on their table, wondering what to make.

"Why don't we forget about wheels," suggested Kirsty, "and make a sailboat instead? We always see such nice ones when we go on vacation. Do you remember, Rachel?"

Rachel's face lit up. She'd never forget the pretty sailboats on Rainspell Island!

"Oh yes!" she exclaimed. "We could use this shoebox as the boat, then cut the sails out of a cereal box."

"I'll cut out the sails," offered Adam.

"And I'll start on the boat," replied Amina, reaching for the shoebox. She'd leaned over to take the box from Rachel when an ugly green hand grabbed the other side.

"I want that!" snapped a goblin voice. "We need it for our rocket!"

Before Rachel and Amina could argue, the goblin had stuffed the shoebox under his arm and scuttled back to his table.

"Let him have it," said Kirsty. "We can use this other box instead."

She reached for the glue, but somehow it tipped over, covering the table and boxes in white goo.

"It's everywhere!" exclaimed Rachel.

The group tried to peel the glue off,
but a lot of the boxes tore and broke into
sticky pieces.

"What a terrible start to making our
boat," groaned Amina.

"Look at my sails," added Adam.
"They're all stuck together in a big
wedge."

Rachel and Kirsty felt their hearts sink. This art class was an absolute disaster! The girls would have to find Alison's missing badge—fast. But where should they start?

Model Magic

While Adam and Amina tried to rescue the sailboat, Rachel and Kirsty moved their chairs closer together.

"We're not the only ones having trouble," Kirsty whispered into her best friend's ear. "Look over there."

Rachel turned to the next table. Dylan, Maya, and Zac were trying to build a model train, but they couldn't get the cars to stick together.

"What's wrong with this glue?" Maya frowned. "It makes my fingers sticky, but it won't work on the cardboard!"

"We have to get Alison's magical star badge back," said Rachel.

"I'll give you three guesses for where to start looking," replied Kirsty, pointing to the goblins' table.

The naughty new boys were working on the tallest model rocket the girls had ever seen. The body was made of several boxes glued together, then painted white. There was a rolled-up

piece of paper at the top for a nose cone
and a row of egg carton engines around
the bottom. There were even windows
and a door hatch cut out of the sides.
As the smug goblins added the finishing
touches, they kept stopping to laugh and
boo at everybody else's mishaps.

Rachel peeked across at the biggest
goblin. Alison's magical star badge must
still be in his pants pocket! Nothing
else would explain his amazing art
project.

"I'm going to wash
my paintbrush," she
said quietly. "That
way I'll be able to
get a closer look
at them."

Rachel pushed

her chair back just
as Mr. Beaker
was walking
past with a
can of green
paint. *Splat!*
Rachel's
elbow knocked
against his
arm, sending the
can spinning across the floor.

"Careful!" he cried.

Tears sprang to Rachel's eyes. "Oh my gosh!" she sobbed. "Mr. Beaker, I am so sorry!"

Mr. Beaker steadied himself, then stepped out of the paint puddle.

"It's OK." He smiled. "It was an accident. Adam and Amina, would you

run to the custodian's office and bring
me a mop and bucket?"

"I'll get some paper towels," said
Kirsty.

The girls tried their best to mop up the
paint with the towels, but there was too
much of it. As Kirsty stepped back to
avoid the green puddle, she skidded on
the slippery floor.

"Watch out!" she
shoulted, sliding
right across
the room.
Kirsty put
out her
hands to
stop herself,
but it was
too late.

Her arm caught the goblins' rocket, knocking it off the table!

"Hey!" screeched the bigger goblin, stepping forward to catch the model just in the nick of time. He instantly turned to his goblin friend and jabbed him in the tummy. "That was all your fault!"

The other goblin was furious. "No it wasn't!" he shouted back.

Kirsty breathed a sigh of relief. The silly pair hadn't realized that *she* had knocked it over!

"Over here!" she whispered to Rachel, ducking behind the boxes on Mr. Beaker's desk.

Rachel rushed over. As soon as the friends were out of sight, Alison flitted out of Rachel's blazer pocket.

"Stay still," she said urgently. "I'm going to turn you into fairies."

Rachel and Kirsty held hands. Suddenly a fountain of fairy dust fizzed all around them, covering them in a sparkling shower of pink and gold.

"It's happening," murmured Rachel. "We're getting smaller!"

Blast Off!

In the blink of an eye, Kirsty and Rachel had shrunk down to fairy size. Kirsty unfurled her delicate wings and smiled. It felt wonderful to be magical again!

"Thank you," gushed Rachel, fluttering over to give Alison a hug.

Alison giggled with pleasure.

"If we're all tiny," she reasoned, "Mr. Beaker won't notice if you take some time away to try to save his art class."

"Let's get closer to those goblins," suggested Kirsty, taking Rachel's and Alison's hands.

The fairies flitted across the classroom as fast as their wings would take them. One by one, they darted into the door hatch cut into the side of the goblins' model rocket. There was just enough room for them to fly up into the center and peek out of the cardboard windows.

Rachel hoped that the goblins wouldn't
see the three little clouds of fairy dust
hanging in the air, but she didn't need to
worry. The cranky new boys were still so
busy arguing, they didn't even notice!

"I wonder where my
badge is," said Alison,
popping her little
head out of the rocket
window.

"It can't be far away,"
answered Rachel.

Suddenly Kirsty had a great idea. She
fluttered up inside the nose cone and,
using all her might, pushed the rolled-up
paper off the top of the rocket.

"Maybe if the rocket needs to be fixed,
the goblins will *have* to use the magical
gold star badge!" she declared.

"Good thinking," agreed Rachel, flying down to the bottom of the rocket. With a giant fairy heave, she managed to push the egg carton engines away from the base.

At that very moment, a deafening shout shook the model from top to bottom.

"What happened here?" roared the bigger goblin, noticing the damage. "Who's been messing with my rocket?"

"Don't start blaming me again," complained his friend.

50

As the bigger goblin picked the rocket up to take a closer look, the loose egg carton engines fell off the bottom. His face turned a horrible purple color.

"It *is* you!" he fumed, pushing the other goblin back on his chair.

The smaller goblin was indignant. "Why would I want to do that?" he argued, before grumbling under his breath, "You probably knocked it off with your big, clumsy hands."

Kirsty, Rachel, and Alison clung to the cardboard walls inside the rocket, their hearts pounding.

"It's obviously not me!" barked the bigger goblin. "How could I mess up the rocket when I have the fairies' magical star badge?"

With that, the goblin pulled Alison's badge out of his pants pocket and waved it in the air.

"This could be our chance," said Alison, pointing out the rocket window.

But suddenly, they found themselves on the move again. Grabbing the broken pieces and some glue in one hand, and the rocket with the fairies inside in the other, the goblin raced across the classroom. He tore right past Amina and Adam with the mop and bucket, straight out of the school building.

"What is he doing now?" cried Kirsty. "Students can't leave class without permission!"

The friends were knocked around terribly as the goblin ran faster and faster. He headed into the playground before finally setting the rocket down. As soon as the model was steady, Alison, Kirsty, and Rachel snuck out of the hatch door and flitted out of sight. With a wave of her wand, Alison turned the girls back to human size.

Kirsty and Rachel ducked behind the jungle gym and waited. Thinking he was alone, the goblin crouched on the ground and started to glue the broken pieces of cardboard back into place.

"This rocket was all my idea," he

muttered. "Wait 'til they see it fly
through the sky!"

As soon as he'd put the model back
together again, the goblin started to
clamber up the jungle gym. Rachel saw
her chance.

"Hey!" she called. "What are you
doing with that amazing rocket?"

The goblin's face broke into a proud
smirk.

"Bet you wish you'd made it!" he taunted. "Look at all the awesome features I've added."

Rachel winked at Kirsty. Goblins really were the vainest creatures in the world! The new boy couldn't resist showing off every detail of his model. While he droned on about how smart he was, Alison fluttered up behind him.

"I think I can get it," she mouthed, pointing to the badge sticking out of the goblin's pocket.

But before Alison could swoop down and take it, a sly look crossed the goblin's face. He rummaged in his pocket, pulled out the badge, and held it up in the air!

Enchanted Skies

"Know what this is?" bragged the goblin, waving the Art Fairy's gold star badge under Rachel's and Kirsty's noses.

Both girls nervously shook their heads. Poor Alison fluttered silently around the back of the goblin, then hid herself in the bib of Kirsty's apron.

"It's a badge, obviously!" continued the new boy. "With this, I can make my rocket fly. And not just some silly little distance, either. This will make it soar right across the playground!"

Rachel summoned up all her courage. She stepped closer, trying to look unimpressed by the goblin's claims.

"If the badge is *really* magic," she challenged, "wouldn't it have to be inside the rocket somewhere to make it fly?"

Irritated, the goblin thought for a minute. Rachel was right! Then he seemed to remember his door hatch.

"Watch this!" he crowed, opening the little door and shoving the magical badge inside. The goblin lifted the rocket high in the air and hurled it up as hard as he could.

"Good job, Rachel!" chimed a silvery voice.

Alison burst out from Kirsty's apron and darted into the air. She waved her wand in a circle, sending starbursts and twinkly paint palettes fizzing in all directions.

"Look at the rocket now," said Rachel, pointing up at the sky.

Alison's magic had sent the model flying in a loop-the-loop, just like the movement of her wand.

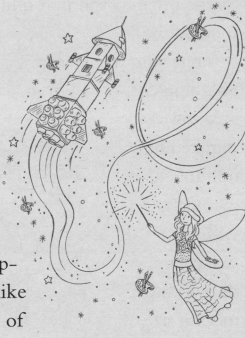

"Are you ready, Kirsty?" she asked, her eyes dancing with excitement.

"Stop it!" barked the goblin.

The rocket arched over the playground before gliding gently down into Kirsty's outstretched hands. Kirsty immediately opened the door hatch and pulled out the magical badge.

"Here you go, Alison." She giggled.

Alison thanked her and touched the badge with her wand. It shrank down to fairy size right away. The

delighted fairy fluttered and somersaulted
above the girls' heads,
filling the air with joyful sparkles
of color.

The goblin swiped
feebly at the fairy,
but he knew his
fun was over.

"You two ruin
everything!" he
shouted, sticking his
tongue out at Kirsty
and Rachel.

"At least you have your
rocket," said Kirsty, handing the model
back to the disgruntled goblin.

"We need to go back inside, Alison,"
called Rachel. "See you soon!"

"Good riddance!" blurted the goblin.

Alison blew the girls a kiss and disappeared into the afternoon sky. Kirsty and Rachel skipped back into class, but the goblin didn't follow them. Instead, he got back to launching his precious toy. He threw the rocket up into the air, but without any fairy magic, it crashed straight back down to the ground again.

By the end of the afternoon, Mr. Beaker's classroom was a much nicer place to be. Other than the grumpy goblin in the corner, everybody was working quietly and happily on their model vehicles.

"He's still out there," whispered Rachel, pointing out the classroom window. The bigger goblin was still storming up and down the playground with his rocket.

"Some goblins never learn." Kirsty chuckled, fitting the mast onto their model boat. She beamed across the table at Adam and Amina. Their vehicle had beautiful rainbow sails, a cabin in the middle, and a row of round portholes.

Mr. Beaker stood up in front of the whiteboard.

"And the winner for best art project is . . . Dylan, Maya, and Zac's terrific passenger train!"

Kirsty and Rachel clapped enthusiastically. The train really did look sensational!

"The vehicle will be displayed in a place of pride in the school lobby," added Mr. Beaker, "in time for the school superintendent's visit."

"But we're not ready for the superintendent yet!" whispered Rachel. "The School Day Fairies are still missing two badges!"

Kirsty held out her pinkie finger, linking it with her best friend's. It was the girls' way of making very special promises to each other.

64

"We'll find those magical badges before I go home," she declared. Kirsty looked determined. The goblins hadn't gotten the best of them yet. "You and I will never give up on the fairies!"

Rachel and Kirsty found Marissa
and Alison's missing magic badges.
Now it's time for them to help

Lydia
the Reading Fairy!

Join their next adventure in
this special sneak peek…

Backward Books

"I love the smell of libraries, don't you?" said Kirsty Tate.

She took a deep breath and looked around at the bookshelves of the Tippington School library. Her best friend, Rachel Walker, smiled at her.

"I love having you here at school with me," she said. "I wish it was for longer than a week!"

It was only the third day of the new school year, and it had already turned into the most fun and exciting time at school that Rachel had ever known. She had lots of friends at Tippington School, but none of them were as special as Kirsty. She had often wished that they could go to the same school. Then Kirsty's school had been flooded, and the repairs were going to take a week. So for five happy days the best friends were at school together at last.

"It's turning into quite a week, though," Kirsty replied with a grin.

Rachel knew that Kirsty was talking about the extraordinary secret they shared. From the time they had met on Rainspell Island, they had been friends of Fairyland. Even though they had often had magical adventures since then, it was always thrilling to meet brand-new fairy friends. And on the first day of this school year, they had been introduced to the School Day Fairies.

"I wonder if we'll see any of the School Day Fairies today," Kirsty whispered.

Before Rachel could reply, her teacher clapped his hands together to get everyone's attention.

RAINBOW magic™

Which Magical Fairies Have You Met?

- ❑ The Rainbow Fairies
- ❑ The Weather Fairies
- ❑ The Jewel Fairies
- ❑ The Pet Fairies
- ❑ The Dance Fairies
- ❑ The Music Fairies
- ❑ The Sports Fairies
- ❑ The Party Fairies
- ❑ The Ocean Fairies
- ❑ The Night Fairies
- ❑ The Magical Animal Fairies
- ❑ The Princess Fairies
- ❑ The Superstar Fairies
- ❑ The Fashion Fairies
- ❑ The Sugar & Spice Fairies
- ❑ The Earth Fairies
- ❑ The Magical Crafts Fairies
- ❑ The Baby Animal Rescue Fairies
- ❑ The Fairy Tale Fairies
- ❑ The School Day Fairies

⌅ SCHOLASTIC

Find all of your favorite fairy friends at
scholastic.com/rainbowmagic

HiT entertainment

RMFAIRY14

RAINBOW magic™

Magical fun for everyone!
Learn fairy secrets, send
friendship notes, and more!

SCHOLASTIC

HiT entertainment

www.scholastic.com/rainbowmagic

RMACTIV4

RAINBOW magic™

SPECIAL EDITION

Which Magical Fairies Have You Met?

- ❑ Joy the Summer Vacation Fairy
- ❑ Holly the Christmas Fairy
- ❑ Kylie the Carnival Fairy
- ❑ Stella the Star Fairy
- ❑ Shannon the Ocean Fairy
- ❑ Trixie the Halloween Fairy
- ❑ Gabriella the Snow Kingdom Fairy
- ❑ Juliet the Valentine Fairy
- ❑ Mia the Bridesmaid Fairy
- ❑ Flora the Dress-Up Fairy
- ❑ Paige the Christmas Play Fairy
- ❑ Emma the Easter Fairy
- ❑ Cara the Camp Fairy
- ❑ Destiny the Rock Star Fairy
- ❑ Belle the Birthday Fairy
- ❑ Olympia the Games Fairy

- ❑ Selena the Sleepover Fairy
- ❑ Cheryl the Christmas Tree Fairy
- ❑ Florence the Friendship Fairy
- ❑ Lindsay the Luck Fairy
- ❑ Brianna the Tooth Fairy
- ❑ Autumn the Falling Leaves Fairy
- ❑ Keira the Movie Star Fairy
- ❑ Addison the April Fool's Day Fairy
- ❑ Bailey the Babysitter Fairy
- ❑ Natalie the Christmas Stocking Fairy
- ❑ Lila and Myla the Twins Fairies
- ❑ Chelsea the Congratulations Fairy
- ❑ Carly the School Fairy
- ❑ Angelica the Angel Fairy
- ❑ Blossom the Flower Girl Fairy
- ❑ Skyler the Fireworks Fairy

3 stories in each one!

📚 SCHOLASTIC

Find all of your favorite fairy friends at
scholastic.com/rainbowmagic

HIT entertainment

RMSPECIAL18